Welcome to ALADDIN QUIX!

If you are looking for fast, fun-to-read stories with colorful characters, lots of kid-friendly humor, easy-to-follow action, entertaining story lines, and lively illustrations, then **ALADDIN QUIX** is for you!

But wait, there's more!

If you're also looking for stories with tables of contents; word lists; about-the-book questions; 64, 80, or 96 pages; short chapters; short paragraphs; and large fonts, then **ALADDIN QUIX** is *definitely* for you!

ALADDIN QUIX: The next step between ready to reads and longer, more challenging chapter books, for readers five to eight years old.

Also by Joan Holub and Suzanne Williams

Goddess Girls series
Heroes in Training series
Thunder Girls series
Little Goddess Girls series
Goddess Girls graphic novels
Heroes in Training graphic novels

School for Magical Monsters series
Book 1: *Rise of Pegasus*
Book 2: *The Eye of Cyclops*

SCHOOL FOR MAGICAL MONSTERS

The Roar of Cerberus

JOAN HOLUB & SUZANNE WILLIAMS
ILLUSTRATED BY TOBY ALLEN

ALADDIN QUIX
New York   Amsterdam/Antwerp   London
Toronto   Sydney/Melbourne   New Delhi

For kids like you who enjoy books with excitement, magic, monsters, and laughs! —Joan and Suzanne

This book is a work of fiction. Any references to historical events, real people, or real places are used fictitiously. Other names, characters, places, and events are products of the author's imagination, and any resemblance to actual events or places or persons, living or dead, is entirely coincidental.

ALADDIN QUIX
Simon & Schuster Children's Publishing Division
1230 Avenue of the Americas, New York, New York 10020
For more than 100 years, Simon & Schuster has championed authors and the stories they create. By respecting the copyright of an author's intellectual property, you enable Simon & Schuster and the author to continue publishing exceptional books for years to come. We thank you for supporting the author's copyright by purchasing an authorized edition of this book.
No amount of this book may be reproduced or stored in any format, nor may it be uploaded to any website, database, language-learning model, or other repository, retrieval, or artificial intelligence system without express permission. All rights reserved. Inquiries may be directed to Simon & Schuster, 1230 Avenue of the Americas, New York, NY 10020 or permissions@simonandschuster.com.
First Aladdin QUIX hardcover edition May 2025
Text © 2025 by Joan Holub and Suzanne Williams
Illustrations © 2025 by Toby Allen
Also available in an Aladdin QUIX paperback edition.
All rights reserved, including the right of reproduction in whole or in part in any form.
ALADDIN and related logo are registered trademarks of Simon & Schuster, LLC.
For information about special discounts for bulk purchases, please contact Simon & Schuster Special Sales at 1-866-506-1949 or business@simonandschuster.com.
Simon & Schuster strongly believes in freedom of expression and stands against censorship in all its forms. For more information, visit BooksBelong.com.
The Simon & Schuster Speakers Bureau can bring authors to your live event. For more information or to book an event contact the Simon & Schuster Speakers Bureau at 1-866-248-3049 or visit our website at www.simonspeakers.com.
Designed by Tiara Iandiorio
The illustrations for this book were rendered digitally.
The text of this book was set in Archer Medium.
Manufactured in the United States of America 0325 LAK
2 4 6 8 10 9 7 5 3 1
Library of Congress Cataloging-in-Publication Data
Names: Holub, Joan, author. | Williams, Suzanne, 1953– author. | Allen, Toby, illustrator.
Title: The roar of Cerberus / by Joan Holub and Suzanne Williams ; illustrated by Toby Allen.
Description: First Aladdin paperback edition. | New York : Aladdin, 2025. | Series: School for magical monsters ; 3 | "A Quix Book." | Audience term: Children | Summary: Cerberus, a three-headed Beast afraid of everything, faces their fears and discovers their hidden courage when they are dared to teach the mysterious Sphinx how to bark. | Identifiers: LCCN 2024040206 (print) | LCCN 2024040207 (ebook) | ISBN 9781665917766 (paperback) | ISBN 9781665917773 (hardcover) | ISBN 9781665917780 (ebook)
Subjects: CYAC: Cerberus (Greek mythology)—Fiction. | Courage—Fiction. | Schools—Fiction. | LCGFT: Mythological fiction. | Classification: LCC PZ7.H7427 Ro 2025 (print) | LCC PZ7.H7427 (ebook) | DDC [Fic]—dc23 | LC record available at https://lccn.loc.gov/2024040206 | LC ebook record available at https://lccn.loc.gov/2024040207

Cast of Characters

CREATURES

Cyclops (SI•clops): tall girl with only one eye and super eyesight

Griffin (GRIFF•en): half-eagle, half-lion boy

Minotaur (MI•no•tohr): boy bull

Pegasus (PEG•uh•suss): boy horse with a white body and wings, who can fly

Sphinx (SFINGKS): girl with a human head, eagle wings, and a lion body

BEASTS

Cerberus (SER•burr•us): three-headed boy dog

Chimera (ky•MEER•uh): girl with a lion head, a goat head, and a dragon head

Flappy: made-up name for one of Cerberus's three heads

Ruff-Ruff: made-up name for one of Cerberus's three heads

Sniffy: made-up name for one of Cerberus's three heads

OTHERS

Hades (HAY•deez): ruler of the Underworld

Mr. Chiron (KI•rawn): schoolteacher centaur (part man, part horse)

shades (SHAYDZ): people in **Greek mythology** who died, then went to the Underworld

Contents

Chapter 1: Three-Headed Dog   1

Chapter 2: Triple-Dog Dare   13

Chapter 3: Shades   25

Chapter 4: Sphinx   39

Chapter 5: Bark and Roar   52

Chapter 6: Riddles   66

Word List   81

Questions   84

Authors' Note   87

Three-Headed Dog

"Arooo! Arooo! Arooo!"

That means "Hello! Hello! Hello to you!" in dog talk. It can also mean "goodbye," "I'm hungry," or something else.

Anyway, as you can see, I'm a

Beast! A three-headed dog with three big-toothed grins and a dragon tail. Scary, right? We dare you to come closer!

Ha! We see you shaking your head no. Good choice. Because if you take our dare, we might bark so loud your ears will hurt!

Our name is **Cerberus**. (You say it like this: *SER-burr-us*.) But each of us dog heads have our own special name too.

"I'm **Sniffy**, the dog head with the best sense of smell."

"I'm **Ruff-Ruff**, the middle and growliest head."

"And I'm **Flappy**. My big ears help me hear really well. And right now, my ears tell me someone is coming." *Clip-clop! Clip-clop!*

It's our teacher, **Mr. Chiron**.

He's a **centaur**—half human and half horse. He's galloping toward us across Mighty Meadow, where we're waiting for him to start class. This grassy, flowery meadow is our outdoor school. Mr. Chiron says that the stuff we learn here will make us mighty!

Wind whips colorful flags atop the tall poles that ring our meadow. The sun is shining. It's a great day. What could go wrong? Plenty, when it comes to Beasts and **Creatures**!

There are six of each here at the School for Magical Monsters. That's twelve students in all. Our school's on **Mount Olympus** and it's **awesome-pawsome**! One teensy problem, though. Beasts and Creatures don't get along. But with our teacher's help, we're all working on it.

"Good morning, students!" Mr. Chiron calls out when he reaches us. He teaches us about all kinds of subjects. One day he gave us tools to make metal sculptures.

Another time we learned to help frowny flowers smile again. *What will it be today?* we all wonder. We soon find out.

"Today will be Make and Do Day!" he tells us. We look at one another, wondering what this means.

"*Making* a friend often happens while *doing* good," he explains. "So that's what Make and Do Day is all about. Making friends while doing good!"

All of us Beasts and Creatures

groan. We can't help it. Because we know what's coming next.

"Today you'll work in six groups," Mr. Chiron says. "One Beast and one Creature on each two-person team."

Argh! Our teacher is always pairing us up like this. To try to get Beasts and Creatures to become better friends. Some days his plan works. Other days not so much.

"In a minute, you'll each choose a teammate," Mr. Chiron goes on. "Then you'll ask your teammate to help you solve a problem. Maybe your teammate needs help making something new or fixing something that's broken. Or maybe they just need someone to listen while they talk about something that's troubling them."

Flappy flaps his big ears. "I've got *two* good listening ears," he whispers proudly.

"When I clap, you'll pair up in teams of two," our teacher says. He raises both hands. *Clap!*

We all look around, wondering

who to choose. Beasts wear beanies with the letter B. Creatures wear caps with a C. Since long ago, Beasts and Creatures have played tricks on each other. Our teacher wants us get along. But trust is hard.

Sniffy nods toward a winged horse named **Pegasus**. "He's okay—for a Creature, that is. Let's ask him to be on our team." But before we can, Pegasus teams up with a Beast named **Chimera**.

Those two are so lucky!

They were the first students to get magic powers. Pegasus's bright white wings are his power. They allow him to fly! Chimera has three heads—lion, goat, and dragon ones. She earned the power to breathe fire. Now she can make yummy s'mores with a fiery blast from her nose.

A Creature named **Cyclops** also got a power. Her magic eyeball lets her see things super close-up! Like the rest of our classmates, we hope to get a power soon too.

"So far, Creatures are doing better than us Beasts when it comes to getting powers," Ruff-Ruff notes.

Flappy nods. "Yeah, it's two against one. Creatures in the lead."

"Today a *Beast* needs to win a power to make it even!" says Sniffy, punching a clawed paw high.

"That's right! A Beast named *Cerberus*!" we say. "Arooo!"

But we all know that magic powers don't just choose a Beast or Creature by chance. Those powers have to be *earned*. Hmm. How can we earn one?

Triple-Dog Dare

"Uh-oh!" says Flappy. "While we've been talking, everyone else chose a teammate." He's right. We look around and notice that everybody's taken. Everybody except—

We gasp. *Oh no!* There's only one student besides us who's not on a team. It's a girl Creature who likes to tell riddles. Hard ones we Beasts can't figure out. She's got a human head, the body of a lion, and two big bird wings.

"What's her name again?" asks Ruff-Ruff.

Sniffy shrugs. "I forget."

"Hmm," says Flappy. "I think it's—"

"**Sphinx**!" we all say. Which rhymes with "stinks." Perfect.

Because she'd *stink* as our partner. She's super smart, it's true, but she likes to rub it in. And we don't like being made to feel stupid. Does anyone?

Sphinx comes over to us. She paws her shiny black hair away from her eyes. "I guess we're on the same

team. So, to help me, here's what you need to do. Ready?"

Uh-oh! What if this is a trap to make us look silly? We can't think of a way out. So we nod.

She pulls a mirror from her pocket. "Mirror, mirror, in my hand. Write the letters I command." She shows us the letters she draws on the mirror: **REWOP CIGAM A.** "So? Can you guess what I want?"

"*GRRR.* We don't like riddles," growls Ruff-Ruff.

Still, we put our heads together and think. Five long minutes later we finally figure it out: **REWOP CIGAM A** is A MAGIC POWER spelled backward!

"Hey! **No fair!**" yells Sniffy. "We can't help you get one of those!"

"Well, you'd better, if you want a good grade. Because a power is what I want," Sphinx says. She crosses her two big wings over her chest.

We dog heads feel tricked.

"Okay, then we want a magic power too," we tell her.

"Nope. **No copycats allowed!**" Sphinx grumps. "Think of something else."

"We're dogs! Not cats!" we yell. "And we want a magic power!"

The other teams hear us shout. Suddenly everyone who doesn't have a power starts asking their teammates for one.

Mr. Chiron clicks his boot heels together to quiet us. "No asking for special powers!" he calls out. "You all know that such powers must be *earned*.

"Try to be your best selves. Instead of arguing, think about ways to make friends. Be helpful and do good, and maybe your power will find *you* today!" It's the same thing he tells us *every* day. So far, no such luck for us dog heads.

Pop! Mr. Chiron disappears, like he often does after giving us schoolwork. But his voice calls out to us. "Oh! The tasks you undertake must be completed tonight before dark," he adds. "I'll *pop* back here then to see how you all did!"

Immediately, Sphinx looks our way. "Okay, so forget the power. Can you guess what I want instead?"

Flappy groans. "Not another riddle!"

"Yeah, guessing games stink," says Sniffy.

"*GRRR*. Just tell us," says Ruff-Ruff.

Sphinx huffs. "You're no fun. But okay. I want you to . . . teach me to bark."

Huh? We dog heads look at each other, surprised. But we're also worried. Because we have a secret nobody knows. We can look scary and act tough. But deep down inside, we're chickens! No, not *real* chickens. It's just that we don't actually know how to bark. We're not brave enough to try. Because barks are scary. Roars, too!

"If Sphinx finds out our secret, she'll tell everyone," Sniffy whispers to Ruff-Ruff and Flappy.

Flappy nods. "Yeah, then no one will think we're brave or scary anymore."

"It'll be so **embarrassing**!" adds Ruff-Ruff.

Luckily, we know a trick to stop our secret from getting out. We'll give Sphinx a dare. Something she can't do. Even if she *is* smart.

"Barking's too easy," we tell Sphinx. "We triple-dog dare you to come up with a harder task. If we *can't* do it, then we'll teach you to bark *and* roar." This seems like a safe dare. Because there's pretty much no task we can't do. Except bark and roar.

"Hmm," says Sphinx. "How about this? You make up three riddles for me. I could use a few new ones. If I answer all three correctly, I win your dare."

Oh no! we think. We're terrible at riddles! Seems like we just made things worse. Still, we say "okay." Because what else can we do?

Shades

"Okay, that's settled," Sphinx says to us dog heads. "Now what is it that you want me to make or do for *you*?"

"Let's think of a really hard task," Ruff-Ruff whispers to Flappy and Sniffy. "If Sphinx doesn't do it, we're off the hook. We won't have to think up riddles. Instead, we'll tell her we both have to come up with new tasks."

While we're thinking hard about a mighty task, a strong wind whips Sniffy's Beast beanie off his head. We all run after it as it tumbles away. Sphinx, too. Through the meadow, over some hills, and into the deep dark cave it rolls.

Whoosh! Sniffy's beanie disappears down a hole in the cave floor.

This cave is creepy. Students are always losing stuff in there. And what gets lost *stays* lost. Because nobody is brave enough to actually go down into that hole.

"My Beast beanie!" cries Sniffy. **"It's gone!"**

Ruff-Ruff nods. "Yeah, Cyclops

told me that she lost a ball in there yesterday."

"And our yellow cape blew into that cave last week, remember?" Flappy reminds us. "I wish we could get everyone's things back."

This gives us an idea. "We triple-dog dare you to go down this hole," Ruff-Ruff tells Sphinx.

"And bring back all the lost stuff down there," adds Sniffy. "That's our Make and Do Day dare!"

"And while you're doing that, we'll think up three riddles no one can answer. Not even you," says Flappy.

We expect her to say no to our dare. And she does. But not in the way we expect.

"NO...problem!" she says. Then she dives into the hole, gently flapping her wings.

We stare after her in surprise. The opening to the cave is deep and dark, so she soon disappears from sight. We can't believe she took us up on our scary dare!

"What if she gets stuck down

there and can't find her way out?" asks Ruff-Ruff.

"It'll be our fault!" Sniffy exclaims.

Flappy twists an ear toward the hole. "Sphinx? You okay?" He leans closer, hoping to hear her reply. *Uh-oh!* This makes us lose our balance. If one of us falls, we all fall, of course, so . . .

down,

down,

down we go.

Thonk! We land at the bottom

of the deep, dark cave. "Oof!" says Flappy as he bumps his ear. "Ow!" growls Ruff-Ruff as he thumps his nose.

Sniffy whacks an elbow. "Oh

no!" he says. "We're trapped at the bottom of the cave!"

"I'm sorry I dragged us all down here!" says Flappy.

"S'okay," says Sniffy. "**Accidents happen.**"

"I can't see anything," whispers Ruff-Ruff.

None of us can. But soon our six eyes get used to the dark. Now we can see a tall golden gate nearby. It glows with light. And there's a sign on it that reads **Underworld**.

But there's no Sphinx, no ball,

no beanie, and no cape down here. We don't spy any of the things other students have lost in this cave either.

Suddenly Flappy points a paw. "**Look!** Over there behind that gate. What are those glowing lights?"

Our eyes get big. Because those lights . . . they're actually glow-in-the-dark humans!

"Who are you?" we call out, backing away.

"We're called **shades**!" they

explain. "Because we're so bright, we've got to wear shades, as in, *sunglasses,* even in the dark. Who are you?"

These glowing shades don't smile. They don't frown. They just stare at us from beyond the gate.

"Wow! You guys glow like big

fireflies," says Sniffy. The shades don't seem too scary. Feeling braver, we move closer.

Flappy sighs. "I wish *we* glowed. Then maybe we could find our way out of this hole."

"I wonder if Mr. Chiron is watching over us right now. Even though we can't see him," says Sniffy.

"Let's hope not. Because we might get in trouble for coming down here," says Flappy.

Sniffy waves an arm toward

the hole high above us. "Duh! We're *already* in trouble! We can't get out of here without a very tall ladder. And we've also lost Sphinx!"

"Oh! I have an idea!" Ruff-Ruff tells Sniffy and Flappy. "Mr. Chiron said that being helpful is a good way to earn a special power. As long as we're down here, maybe we can somehow help these shades."

The best thing about having three heads? One of us can almost always come up with a good idea like this one!

We step up to the tall golden gate and smile wide. "Need any help?" we ask the shades on the other side of its bars.

Sphinx

The shades back away fast. "Why are you looking at us like that?" they ask in alarm.

"We're just smiling," growls Ruff-Ruff.

"**Well, stop it.** Your

smiles are scary!" says one shade.

"And your teeth are big and sharp! **I bet you want to eat us!**" yells another shade.

Sniffy shakes his head. "No, we don't. We just had breakfast an hour ago. We only want to help you."

"Really?" says a third shade. "Then help us get out of here. We, um, are late to a party. Because we accidentally got locked inside this gate."

"Sure! We'll try," says Flappy.

Ruff-Ruff points to the big lock on the gate. "Yeah, just give us the key to that lock," he suggests.

"We don't *have* the key!" says a shade. "If we did, we'd unlock the gate ourselves. You guys are not very bright, are you?"

"Luckily, you shades glow brightly enough for all of us to see down here," jokes Sniffy. All three of us dog heads giggle. But the shades just look grumpy.

"What if we stick our strong tail between the bars of this gate?"

Flappy says to the shades. "You could all climb on. Then, with a flick of our tail, we'll boost you up and over the top of the gate!"

"Good plan!" agree the shades.

Quickly we dog heads poke our long, strong tail between the gate's bars. The shades all climb onto our tail. We give them a big push upward. *Whoosh!* Up to the top of the tall gate they go! Soon they're sliding down the outside of the gate's bars. They land safely on the ground beside us. Then, to

our surprise, they all run away!

"**Wait!** You didn't even thank us!" Ruff-Ruff calls after them.

"Never mind. We helped those shades. That's what counts," says Sniffy. "So any minute now, we should get our special power!"

While we're waiting to get our

power, we sing a song. It goes like this: "One little, two little, three little dog heads." We sing it over and over. That's all the words in the whole song because we're not real good at making up songs.

"Nothing's happening," Ruff-Ruff says after a while. "Guess this means we won't get a power after all."

Flappy's ears droop. "Yeah, we must not have helped the shades enough. But we *tried* to. That should be worth something."

Sniffy sniffs the air. "Hey! I smell someone heading our way. Someone with a human head, a lion's body, and two big bird wings. Someone carrying a big box."

"It's Sphinx!" yells Ruff-Ruff. "Good thing those shades left some of their light behind, so it's not too dark to see her."

"What are you doing down here?" Sphinx asks when she reaches us. "Never mind. Look what I found! This box is full of stuff we and our friends lost!" She sets the box on the ground and we all look inside it.

Sniffy grins. "Hey! Here's my Beast beanie!" He pulls it out and puts it on.

"And here's that ball Cyclops lost!" says Flappy. He grabs it and tosses it up and down a few times.

Ruff-Ruff digs around in the box, then pulls out a big square of yellow cloth. "Look! I found our cape! There are all kinds of lost things in here that belong to us Beasts and Creatures!"

Sphinx folds her wings. Then she cackle-laughs. "Maybe if you dig deep enough, you'll even come up with those riddles you owe me! Don't forget—if I guess all three of them correctly, you must teach me how to bark and roar."

"Yeah, we know," we say, rolling our eyes. (Though till now we actually *did* forget about the riddles we owe her.) Putting our heads together, we try to come up with three good ones she *won't* be able to answer!

While we're thinking, Sphinx reaches into the box. She pulls out something tiny the size of a teardrop. "I remember this," she says. "It is a gold seed a Creature named **Griffin** made for one of our school **projects**." Next, she pulls out a pointed cone that looks like a party hat. "And here's **Minotaur**'s bullhorn," she says. "I didn't even know he'd lost it!"

Ten minutes later, we dog heads have come up with one riddle each. But will any of them stump Sphinx? Or will she guess their answers right away?

"First riddle," Ruff-Ruff says to Sphinx. "What kind of dog loves bubble baths?"

"A shampoodle!"

Sphinx answers quickly.

Uh-*oh*. We three dog heads look at each other, worried. Because she's really good at guessing!

"Okay, second riddle," says Flappy. "Why is a tree like a dog?"

"Easy peasy," shouts Sphinx, swishing her tail. "Because they both have lots of *bark*!"

We groan. We only have one chance left to trip her up. If Sphinx guesses the answer to our third riddle, she'll win this contest! We'll have to teach her to bark and roar. And when she discovers we're too scared to even try, our embarrassing secret won't be a secret anymore!

Bark and Roar

"Hey! You!" calls a voice. We spot a boy wearing a black cape. He's on the other side of the golden gate from us. Quickly he pulls a big key from his pocket. *Click!* He unlocks the gate, steps out, and walks up to us.

"I'm **Hades**, ruler of the Underworld," he tells us. (He says his name like this: *HAY-deez*.) "I'm looking for some glowing human shades. You didn't open the gate to the Underworld and let them out, I hope?"

"Well, no. But we did boost them up so they could climb *over* the gate," Ruff-Ruff admits.

"Because they said they were late for a party," adds Sniffy.

Sphinx listens, probably trying to figure out what we're all talking about.

Hades frowns. **"Oh no!** Those shades are always trying to make trouble in the outside world. That's why I keep them locked up in the Underworld."

"So they weren't really late to a party?" guesses Flappy.

"No. There *is* no party. They tricked you," said Hades. "They're **sneaky** that way. One time they stood on each other's shoulders and climbed over my gate. It took me forever to find them and put them back in the Underworld. After that, I built a taller gate with a better lock."

"**Sorry!** We didn't know. We thought we were helping," Sniffy tells Hades.

Our shoulders sag. "No wonder we didn't earn a special power," says Ruff-Ruff. "We really messed up!"

"**Hey!**" Just then Sphinx points one of her wingtips toward a very large rock not far away. A bright glow shines from behind it. "Could your shades be hiding back there?" she asks Hades.

All four of us follow Hades as he tiptoes over to the big rock. We all peek around it. And we find the shades! Their arms are full of toys,

kites, ribbons, and other stuff.

"Aha! You've been stealing again, haven't you?" yells Hades. Right away, those shades turn toward us in surprise.

"Maybe," replies one shade. They all laugh.

Hades crosses his arms. "When anything on Earth gets lost, it falls down here into my cave—the Underworld. Sneaky shades hide the lost things and keep them for themselves."

He waves to the shades. "Come

on. Back to the Underworld! Then I'll return all those things you stole from Earth."

But the shades just giggle at Hades. They drop the stuff they're holding and run off. It's like they think stealing is a fun game!

Hades runs after them, trying to round them up. But the shades don't pay him any attention.

To help Hades, Sphinx gathers objects the shades left behind. She puts them in the box to take back to Earth.

We dog heads want to help Hades too. We're faster, so we race past him, catch up to the shades, and growl loudly.

"We're not scared of *you*!" they say, giggling louder.

We frown and open our three mouths to show off our sharp teeth. The shades just laugh harder. "You may *look* scary, but you don't *sound* scary!" they say.

Now we're madder than ever. We yell, "Stealing is not okay! Back to the Underworld, shades!"

Then, all at once, sounds we've never made before blast out of our three mouths.

"BARK! BARK! BARK! *ROARRR!*"

The shades stop in their tracks. Their eyes get huge. They cover their ears.

Ruff-Ruff looks at Flappy and Sniffy. "Wow! I think we just got a magic power!"

"A *bark* power!" says Flappy.

"And a *roar* power too!" adds Sniffy.

"**Yikes!** You guys are loud!" says one shade.

"*Scary* loud," says another shade.

"Run to the Underworld!" shouts a third. "We'll be safe there!" The shades zoom back through the open gate.

We dog heads run over and shut it behind them. *Clink!*

Hades catches up to us and locks the gate. *Click!*

"Wow! Thank you," he tells us. "Without your help, it would've taken me hours to round them all up."

Then he cocks his head at us. "Hey! I just got an idea! I could use a scary three-headed watchdog like you. To guard this gate on weekends when I'm busy in other parts of the Underworld."

We dog heads look at one another and nod. "That sounds like fun!" we say. "We go to school on weekdays. But if our teacher says it's okay, we'll come here on weekends."

"Fantastic!" says Hades. "Later, then."

We smile at him and wave goodbye. We've never felt so good!

But then Sphinx comes over

carrying the box of stolen stuff. She sets it down and says, "Okay . . . now, ask me riddle number three."

Riddles

We three dog heads look at one another. If Sphinx figures out our last riddle, she wins our dare. She'll want us to teach her to bark and roar! How can we teach her when we only just learned these things ourselves? Oh well, here goes nothing...." Okay, here's our third riddle," Sniffy mutters. "What walks on four legs first. Then two legs next. Then three legs last?"

Sphinx frowns. "Hmm. That's

a hard one." She gets quiet. She walks back and forth, thinking. After a minute, her wings droop. "I give up," she says.

We can hardly believe our good luck!

"So, what's the answer?" Sphinx asks us.

"A human!" we tell her. Then we explain our riddle.

"Before it can walk, a human baby crawls on two hands and two legs. Which kind of equals *walking* on *four* legs," says Ruff-Ruff.

"But when a human gets old enough, it walks upright. On *two* legs," adds Sniffy.

"And toward the end of its life, a human might need to use a cane. To steady its two legs while walking," says Flappy. "So that sort of equals *three* legs. Get it?"

Sphinx's eyes light up. "Yes! Wow, that's a great riddle! Can I borrow it?" she asks us.

We look at her in surprise. "What for?"

"To protect the **Egyptian pyramids**. Pyramids are monuments for Egyptian kings called **pharaohs**. They're full of riches like art and gold. I try to keep thieves away from the pyramids," she tells us. "But often I'm too busy with school. So I was wondering . . . could I write your riddle on all the pyramids' front doors?"

"How would that help?" asks Flappy.

"Well, if someone reads your

riddle, but can't answer it—" Sphinx begins.

"They won't be able to go inside the pyramid?" guesses Ruff-Ruff.

"Right!" says Sphinx. "The correct answer acts like a key. The doors won't open without it."

"And our riddle would keep the pyramids safe from bad guys," says Sniffy. "'Cause it's a really, really hard one!"

"Yes, you can borrow our riddle," we tell her.

"Thanks so much!"

Sphinx claps her wings. "Now, c'mon. We've been down here a long time. Climb on my back and I'll fly us outta here."

We climb on, holding the box of lost objects between us. *Flap! Flap!* Up to the top of the hole and out of the deep dark cave we fly!

After Sphinx lands outside and we climb down, we all four walk back to Mighty Meadow. It's afternoon now. Most of our classmates have already gathered there.

Mr. Chiron arrives. Suddenly

our beanies and Sphinx's cap all start to twinkle.

"W-what's happening?" she wonders.

"I think you just got your magic power!" Flappy tells her. "Not a power that we can see like Pegasus's wings. I think yours must be the kind you can't see. **A *helping* power!**"

"Yeah! Because you got the idea to *help* protect the pyramids," Sniffy tells Sphinx.

"And you *helped* gather those

stolen objects and got us out of that cave," adds Ruff-Ruff.

"Your beanies twinkled too, though, Cerberus," says Sphinx. "What power did you get?"

When we don't say anything, she takes a guess. "You dog heads learned to bark and roar *today*, didn't you? When you sent those shades back to the Underworld. That's when you earned your power! Your power can't be seen, either. But it can sure be heard!"

Whoa! Sphinx figured it out.

She really *is* good at guessing!

"No one at school knew you couldn't bark and roar," Sphinx goes on. "I sure didn't. You usually say you don't feel like barking. Or you're too busy to roar."

"Yeah, but that wasn't true. We were just too chicken to do either. Please don't tell," we dog heads ask her.

Sphinx stares at us, then nods and says, "Okay, but I have one last riddle for you."

We roll our eyes. Though in

truth, we don't mind her riddles anymore. They're kind of fun. "Okay. We're listening," we say.

She grins. "If you don't keep it, it'll break. What is it?"

We three dog heads think and think and think. And then, all six of our eyes light up. "A promise?" we guess.

"Right!" Sphinx grins. "And here's a *promise* I'll never break: I will keep your secret. You were so brave today, helping Hades. And you earned bark and roar powers to loudly and proudly show your bravery. You stood up to those sneaky, stealing shades and chased them back to the Underworld!"

"***Arooo! Arooo! Arooo!*** Thanks!" we tell her.

We all smile as we walk across the meadow toward the other Beasts and Creatures. Right away, we return everyone's lost things. And tell them what happened with Hades and the shades. When the four of us share our big news about getting helping powers, our schoolmates cheer.

This morning the magic powers score was Creatures, 2, and Beasts, 1. Now the score is Creatures, 3, and Beasts, 2. The

Creatures are still ahead. But that's okay. There's lots of time for us Beasts to catch up!

It has been a wonderful day for us dog heads! We had a fun adventure and earned our special power. But best of all, we made *two* new friends—Sphinx and Hades!

Word List

accidents (AK·sih·dents): Mistakes

Beast (BEEST): A young monster who wears a beanie with a B

centaur (SEHN·tahr): A creature who is part man and part horse

Creature (KREE·cher): A young monster who wears a cap with a C

Egyptian pyramids (ee·JIP·shun PEER·uh·mihdz): Ancient structures built of large stones

embarrassing (em•BARE•uh•sing): Something that makes a person feel uncomfortable, shy, and/or ashamed

Greek mythology (Greek mith•AH•lo•jee): Stories that people in the country of Greece made up long ago to explain things they didn't understand about their world

Mount Olympus (mownt oh•LIM•pus): The tallest mountain in Greece

pharaohs (FAY•rowz): Ancient Egyptian kings

projects (PRAH•jekts): Tasks or work to do

sneaky (SNEE•key): Sly or tricky

Underworld (UN•der•world): The place where people in Greek mythology went after they died

Questions

1. Which Cerberus dog head do you think would be the most fun to be? Why?
2. Draw a picture of yourself as a magical monster. Use your imagination to make your monster self scary, silly, or funny—or all those things together! Are you a Beast or a Creature? What is your monster name?

3. If you went to the School for Magical Monsters, what kind of magic power would you hope for?
4. Cerberus doesn't want to tell Sphinx he can't bark and roar. That's partly because he's embarrassed that he can't do either. If you had a friend who was embarrassed about something they couldn't do, how would you help? What could you do or say to give them more confidence or help

them feel better about their abilities?

5. Can you think of a dog (or some other animal) riddle to tell Sphinx?

Authors' Note

Hi! We are Joan and Suzanne, two friends who have fun writing books together. Our inspiration for the Creatures, Beasts, and other characters in the books comes from Greek mythology.

Cerberus, for example, is a three-headed dog. In mythology, he guards the gate to the Underworld for Hades. And Sphinx tells riddles to keep visitors away from the pyramids of Egypt.

In the School for Magical Monsters series, we bring these mythological characters together and let them discover their magic powers.

We hope you have fun reading all the School for Magical Monsters books!

—Joan Holub and Suzanne Williams